Wishing you marvellous things
and MAGIC! !

Kristina Stephenson
x

THE MUSEUM OF
MARVELLOUS THINGS

KRISTINA STEPHENSON

Hodder
Children's
Books

Sensible, serious Norbert Norris knew all the important things . . .

Like the name of EVERY dinosaur and all the planets in the sky, and that when a camel only has one hump it's called a d-r-o-m-e-d-a-r-y.

He knew about:

sums 4+6+8

and sizing shapes

and sounding out REALLY BIG words.

Per-pen-dic-u-lar

Yes, Norbert Norris TOTALLY knew ALL the important things.

Then, one day, to his surprise, an invitation
flew through his window:

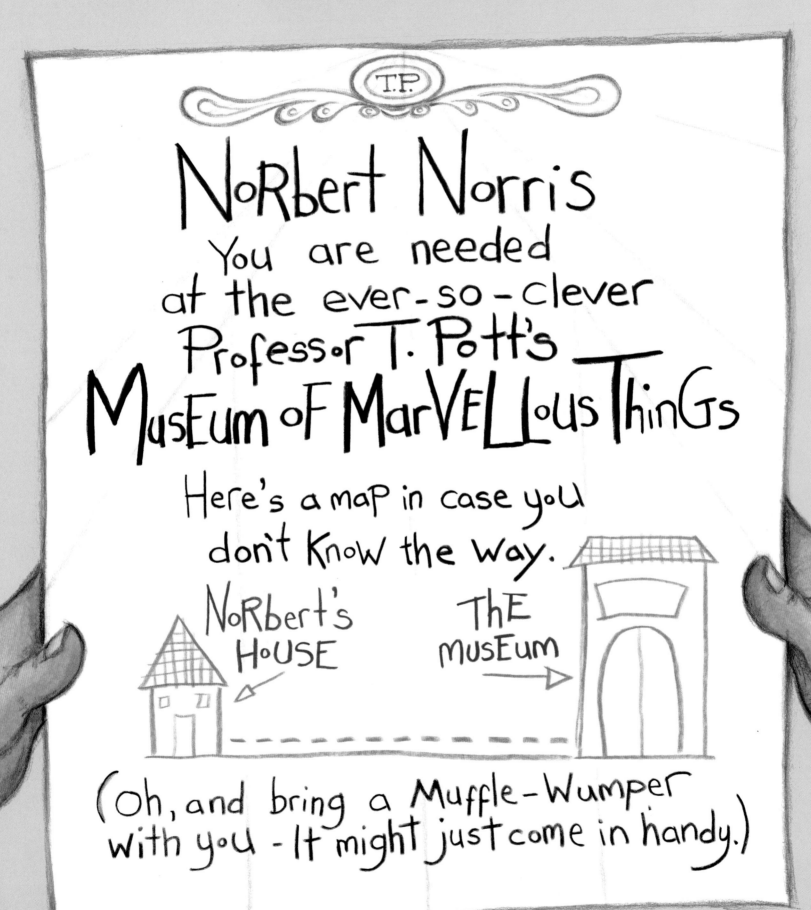

T.P.

NoRbert Norris

You are needed
at the ever-so-clever
Professor T. Pott's
MuseEum of MarVELLous ThinGs

Here's a map in case you
don't Know the way.

NoRbert's
HoUSE

ThE
muSEum

(Oh, and bring a Muffle-Wumper
with you - It might just come in handy.)

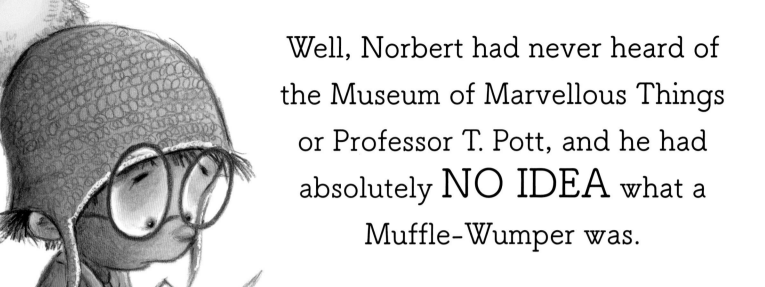

Well, Norbert had never heard of the Museum of Marvellous Things or Professor T. Pott, and he had absolutely NO IDEA what a Muffle-Wumper was.

But he *did* LOVE museums, so he grabbed his favourite backpack, and headed out the door.

It didn't take long for Norbert to get to the Museum of Marvellous Things.

Norbert's House

The museum was

HUMONGOUS!

And there in the hall,
where Norbert thought a
diplodocus ought to be . . .

. . . a dragon
with a flagon
was standing by a
wagon, staring at
a bubbling brew.

"How silly!"
said sensible, serious
Norbert Norris.
"Why would anyone put
that in a museum?"

Professor
T. Pott will
know what's
what.

Norbert thought he'd heard a
voice, but no one else was there . . .

Next,
Norbert and his
favourite backpack
set off up the stairs.

There were stars in jars and moons like balloons.

Professor T. Pott will know what's what.

"That's odd!" said sensible, serious Norbert Norris.

Again he heard the voice, but there still wasn't anyone there.

Instead he saw:

Doo-Dahs
in cages,

Noo-Nahs on stages,

and a Numpkin with
only one hump.

He found:

a carpet that flew,

five fairies,

a Hoo,

and four books in a terrible GRUMP.

"I DON'T
UNDERSTAND
THIS PLACE!"
cried Norbert.

But just at that moment . . .

"Welcome to the Museum of Marvellous Things!
I'm so pleased to see you, Norbert Norris!"

"I'm Tilly Pott," said the little girl. "The ever-so-clever Professor T. Pott was my great, great, great grandfather. He built this museum a long time ago with the magic of his imagination, and *I* look after it now. But the museum's in terrible trouble . . . It's running out of magic and soon everything will disappear!"

"Then, why don't you make some *more* magic?" said Norbert.

"I don't know how to," said Tilly
"You know ALL the important things. That's
why I need *you* Norbert Norris!"

"But I don't know about magic!"
said Norbert.

Then he felt a tap on his shoulder
and turned his head to see . . .

. . . his favourite backpack – and it was talking!

"The answer is hidden somewhere around here. You just need to look for it," said the Muffle-Wumper.

And that's just what they did!
Norbert and Tilly
swooped and
looped around
Num-Num Trees,
past a Pobble
with purple hair.

They looked under Grimbles
and Grumbles and Gonks.
But the answer wasn't there.

They peered into cases and ALL sorts of places where they thought the answer might be.

From the swirling, whirling Rainbow Room,

to the bottom of the Impossible Sea.

Then . . .

"Look!" cried Tilly.

"The Doo-Dahs!
The Noo-Nahs!

The Fairies!
The Hoo!

Everything in the museum
is about to disappear."

"But, this place is
AMAZING!" said
Norbert Norris.
"We TOTALLY
have to save it."

"How?" said Tilly.
"We don't know the
answer."

"It's all about

MAGIC!"

said the Muffle-Wumper.
"So, think of the *most* magical thing in the world."

"But I DON'T KNOW ABOUT MAGIC!"
cried Norbert.

Then, just as the museum was about to vanish,
he had a very unexpected idea. And Norbert
Norris did something he'd NEVER
done before . . .

He made a WISH! A wish
that the Museum of Marvellous Things
would never EVER disappear.
The wish took flight and the
museum filled with . . .

MAGIC!

You see, when you imagine incredible things, almost anything can happen.

"I knew you could do it, Norbert Norris,"
said the Muffle-Wumper.
"You knew about magic all along."

"Thank you Norbert Norris
for saving the museum,"
said Tilly.

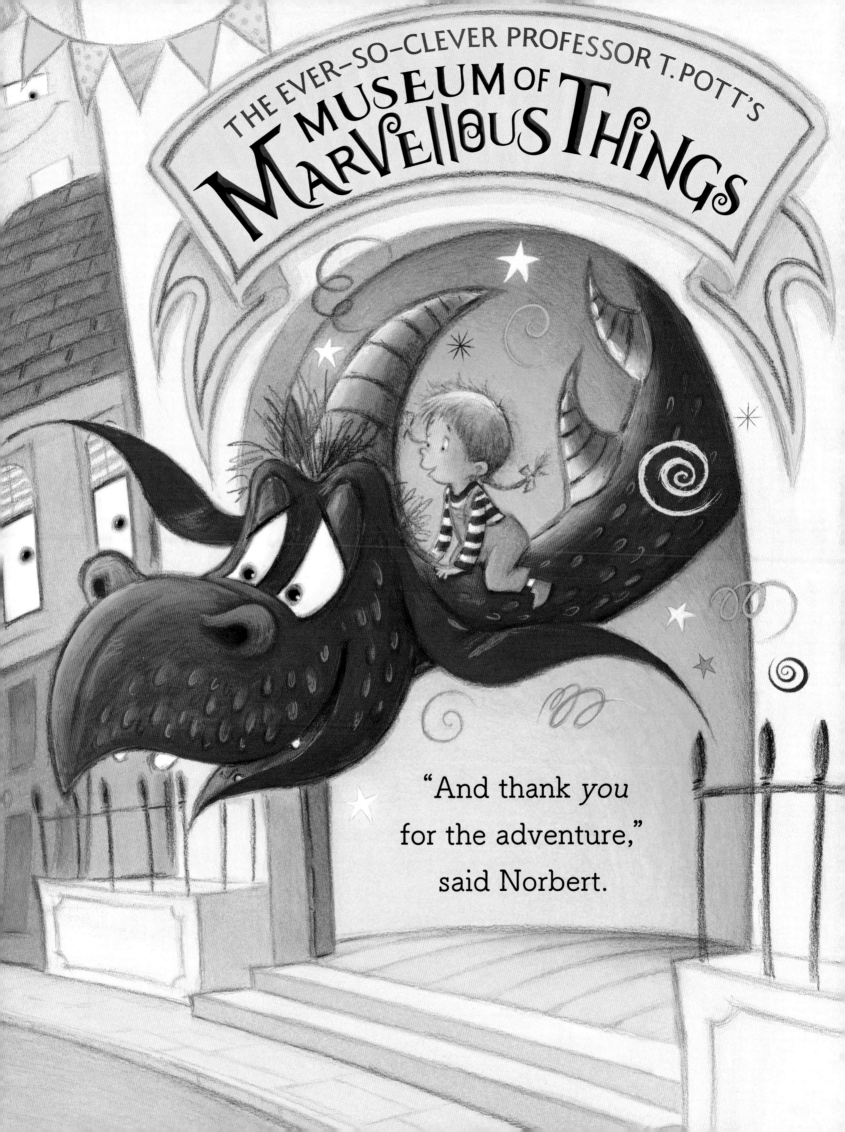

THE EVER-SO-CLEVER PROFESSOR T. POTT'S

MUSEUM OF MARVELLOUS THINGS

"And thank *you*
for the adventure,"
said Norbert.

Norbert Norris
still knew about:
sums and sizing
shapes and sounding
out REALLY BIG
words. But now his
world was full of
MAGIC!

And that, thought Norbert Norris, was the most **marvellous** thing of all!

For Jennifer Stephenson, the brilliant designer of
this book, who TOTALLY knows about magic.
With thanks and love K.S.

HODDER CHILDREN'S BOOKS

First published in Great Britain in 2021
by Hodder and Stoughton

Text and illustration copyright
© Kristina Stephenson, 2021

A CIP catalogue record for this book
is available from the British Library.

HB ISBN: 978 1 444 94604 8
PB ISBN: 978 1 444 94602 4

1 3 5 7 9 10 8 6 4 2

Printed and bound in China

MIX
Paper from
responsible sources
FSC® C104740
FSC
www.fsc.org

Hodder Children's Books, an imprint
of Hachette Children's Group,
part of Hodder and Stoughton,
Carmelite House,
50 Victoria Embankment,
London, EC4Y 0DZ

An Hachette UK Company

www.hachette.co.uk

www.hachettechildrens.co.uk